S0-CFK-951

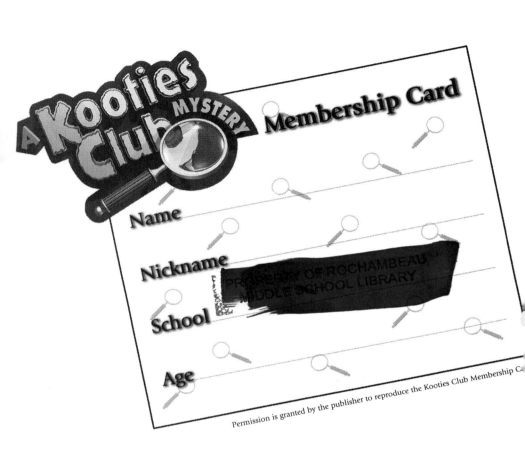

A Kooties Club MYSTERY

Membership Card

Name

Nickname

School

Age

The Mystery of Mr. Dodge

by M. J. Cosson

COVER-TO-COVER BOOKS

Perfection Learning® CA

Cover and Inside Illustrations: Michael A. Aspengren

For information, contact
Perfection Learning® Corporation,
1000 North Second Avenue, P.O. Box 500,
Logan, Iowa 51546-1099.
Paperback 0-7891-2299-5
Cover Craft® 0-7807-7269-5
7 8 9 10 PP 08 07 06 05 04 03

Table of Contents

Introduction 6

Chapter 1. The Mystery 10

Chapter 2. Looking for Clues 16

Chapter 3. Putting the Clues Together . . . 24

Chapter 4. The Dog Search 29

Chapter 5. The Gift 34

Chapter 6. Kim Helps 41

Chapter 7. A Cat Named Dog 47

Chapter 8. Mystery Solved 51

Introduction

Abe, Ben, Gabe, Toby, and Ty live in a large city. There isn't much for kids to do. There isn't even a park close by.

Their neighborhood is made up of apartment houses and trailer parks. Gas stations and small shops stand where the parks and grass used to be. And there aren't many houses with big yards.

Ty and Abe live in an apartment complex. Next door is a large vacant lot. It is full of brush, weeds, and trash. A path runs across the lot. On the other side is a trailer park. Ben and Toby live there.

Across the street from the trailer park is a big gray house. Gabe lives in the top apartment of the house.

The five boys have known each other since they started school. But they haven't always been friends.

The other kids say the boys have cooties. And the other kids won't touch them with a ten-foot pole. So Abe, Ben, Gabe, Toby, and Ty have formed their own club. They call it the Kooties Club.

Here's how to join. If no one else will have anything to do with you, you're in.

The boys call themselves the Koots for short. Ben's grandma calls his grandpa an *old coot*. And Ben thinks his grandpa is pretty cool. So if he's an old coot, Ben and his friends must be young koots.

The Koots play ball and hang out with each other. But most of all, they look for mysteries to solve.

Chapter 1

The Mystery

"Help! Save me!"

"It's too late for you, Jack. You've done it to yourself this time."

"Eeeeeeeeee!" Thud!

"Well, that's the last we'll see of him. He's like a dead bug on a car window now."

"Tell me, Mike, how did you know he did it?"

"Easy. He was sloppy. Jack was mad at Smith because he cut Jack out

of the deal. So Jack made it look like Smith was robbed."

The voice continued. "Then Jack put the money back in the bank. He used a fake name.

"When I showed the bank teller Jack's picture, she said he was the one. Pretty dumb work."

"Well, it was pretty smart of you to figure it out."

The ending music played. Mr. Dodge reached to turn off the tape player.

"Boy, that was good," said Gabe. The other Koots agreed.

"It reminds me of a case I had once," said Mr. Dodge. "The guy killed his partner. Then he tried to make it look as if they had both been robbed."

11

"How did you catch him?" asked Ty.

"We didn't think it was him right away," said Mr. Dodge. "But like all bad guys, he left a trail.

"After things cooled down, he took a trip. It was a very nice trip. It cost more than he made in a year. Sounded fishy.

"I started digging around," Mr. Dodge went on. "I found out he was spending lots of money. Money he shouldn't have had. I kept digging. The money trail led back to the partner. That did it."

"Wow!" said Abe. "Your police work must have been fun."

"Well, fun isn't the word I'd use," said Mr. Dodge. "It was interesting. That's why I like to listen to these

12

mystery stories. I like to guess the ending before it comes."

"Can you do that?" asked Toby.

"Yes. Most of the time I can," answered Mr. Dodge.

"I never know what the ending will be," said Gabe. "I'd like to learn how to do that."

"Just read, listen to, and watch mysteries," said Mr. Dodge. "Find the clues. Put them together. Pretty soon you'll be a pro.

"I have another mystery on tape that I haven't heard. If it's raining again tomorrow, come over after school. We'll listen to it."

"Okay," said all the Koots. They liked listening to the tapes. And they liked Mr. Dodge's stories even better.

"Can we come even if it's sunny?" asked Abe.

"Sure thing. I'll see you guys tomorrow," said Mr. Dodge.

"Bye," said the Koots as they left Mr. Dodge's apartment. "See you tomorrow."

They walked down the stairs. Ben said, "I wonder what happened to Mr. Dodge. Why is he blind? And why can't he walk?"

"It wouldn't be very nice to ask," said Abe.

"We know that, Abe," said Toby.

"Why is he always on the phone?" asked Ty. "What does he do all day?"

"It wouldn't be nice to ask," said Abe.

"We know that, Abe," said Gabe.

14

"I wonder if he has any family," said Ben.

"It . . ." said Abe.

"We know, Abe!" the whole Kooties Club yelled.

"So how can we find out?" asked Toby.

"Spy!" said Gabe.

The Koots were always ready for a good mystery.

Chapter 2

Looking for Clues

The next afternoon, the Koots climbed the stairs to apartment A-13. Mr. Dodge opened the door.

The boys sat in their usual places. Mr. Dodge turned on the tape player. The opening music started.

A printout sat by the phone. Gabe wanted to look at it more closely.

Very quietly, Gabe crept to the phone. Later, the Koots all said they hadn't heard him at all.

But Mr. Dodge could. He looked right at Gabe. He said, "Do you want something, Gabe? There are some cookies in the kitchen. Why don't you bring them out here?"

"Okay," said Gabe. He was shocked. How had Mr. Dodge known it was him moving?

Gabe got the cookies. He passed them around.

After a while, Ty tried to creep over to the printout. Mr. Dodge said, "You know where the bathroom is, Ty. You're welcome to use it. Don't be shy."

17

Ty said, "Thank you." He went into the bathroom. And he didn't even have to! He flushed the toilet. He ran the water. He knew Mr. Dodge could hear everything.

The tape was called *The Mystery of the Walking Body.* It was about a body that kept turning up. Someone would report a murder. The police would come to check it out. But it would be the same body as before.

No one could figure out how the same body kept turning up. A dog finally solved the mystery.

It seems that the killer had a key to the place where dead bodies were kept. Every night he came and took the same body. Then he left it in another place. He wanted to confuse the police.

The last time they brought the body back, the police gave the dog the scent. The dog traced the scent to the killer.

The Koots just sat quietly until the mystery was over. They looked around the room. But they couldn't see much from their seats.

"Boy, that's a smart dog," said Ben.

"I wish I could have a dog like that," added Toby. "But my mom won't let me."

"I wish I could have a dog too," sighed Mr. Dodge. "It would be good company."

"Why don't you get one?" asked Ty. "You can keep pets in these apartments. A dog named Lucky used to live right downstairs. And a dog named Ajax."

19

"I know I can keep one here," said Mr. Dodge. "But I couldn't take care of a dog. I'd have to walk it several times a day. It's a big deal for me to get out every other week."

"I didn't know you ever went out," said Toby.

"Yes. A friend comes for me every other Wednesday. He takes me to the store or to the doctor. And he takes me to get new mystery tapes at the library. We have lunch too.

"You boys are in school then. That's why you never see me outside."

"Anyway, that was a good story, wasn't it?" added Mr. Dodge. "I know it was a good story because I didn't guess the ending."

"Wow! That was a good story!" said Ty.

Just then the doorbell rang. It was a man bringing Meals on Wheels to Mr. Dodge.

Ben opened the door and took the tray. He handed it to Mr. Dodge.

"Guess we'd better be going," he said.

"Thanks for a good story, Mr. Dodge," said Toby.

"Yeah, thanks," said the rest of the Kooties Club. They filed out of the apartment. The door shut behind the boys.

22

Gabe said, "Man, I didn't get one good clue."

"Shhh," said Ben. He walked away from the door. "Remember how good his hearing is," he whispered. "Let's go downstairs."

Abe whispered, "Let's go to my place. Just in case."

They went inside Abe's room. Abe shut the door quietly.

Gabe said, "I think it's okay now, Abe. I don't think Mr. Dodge's hearing is that good."

They all laughed.

Chapter 3

Putting the Clues Together

The Koots sat around Abe's room. Toby said, "We learned one new thing about Mr. Dodge. He goes out every other Wednesday."

"We learned more than that," said Ben. "We learned that a friend takes him. He must not have any family close by."

"We learned something else," said Ty. "He would like to have a dog."

Just then the bedroom door opened. Abe's little sister Kim walked in. Abe shared the room with Kim. So she had the right to come in.

"I know where there's a free cat," Kim said.

"So what else is new?" asked Ty. "There's always a free cat around here."

"But this one has had shots," said Kim. "And she's really nice. She's fixed too."

"What do you mean fixed?" asked Abe.

"I don't know," said Kim. "But it sounds like something good."

"It means she can't have babies," said Gabe. All the Koots hooted.

Kim backed out the door. She didn't want to talk about babies with the Kooties Club.

"Good going!" said Abe. He flashed a big grin. "You got rid of her." The Koots laughed again.

Abe's mom stuck her head in the door. "You boys be nice to Kim," she said. "By the way. It's time for dinner. Time for you boys to head home."

"Let's play ball after supper," said Ben.

"Okay. Meet in the parking lot in half an hour," said Toby. All the Koots agreed.

Later, the Koots took over the parking lot. They kicked a ball back and forth.

After a while, Ben stopped playing.
He sat down on the curb. The other
Koots sat down too.

"What's wrong?" asked Toby.

"I'm just thinking about Mr.
Dodge," whispered Ben.

"Want to go back to my room?"
asked Abe.

"No," said Ty. "Your dumb little
sister will spy on us. Anyway, Mr.
Dodge can't hear us all the way down
here."

"Just in case, whisper," suggested
Gabe.

"Anyway, I was thinking about Mr.
Dodge," whispered Ben. "He should
have a dog. He must get lonely."

"But he can't take care of a dog,"
whispered Toby.

"Maybe we could help him," offered Ben. "Nobody here has a dog. If Mr. Dodge got one, we could all have a dog. We could all help walk him and feed him. And the dog would be all of ours."

"Good idea!" shouted Abe.

"Shhh!" said all the Koots.

Chapter 4

The Dog Search

The next day was Saturday. The Kooties Club met at Ben's trailer.

"Does anybody know where we can get a dog?" asked Toby.

"Nope," said Ty.

"Nope," added Ben.

"Nope," sighed Gabe.

"Nope," said Abe.

"Me neither," said Toby.

"We could look in the paper. The want ads tell about pets," suggested Ben.

"The only paper I have is from last Sunday," he offered. "I guess we could check that."

The want ads didn't have any ads for free dogs.

"Do you think Mr. Dodge would buy a dog?" asked Gabe.

"Then it wouldn't be a gift from us," said Ty.

"Then it wouldn't be a surprise," said Ben.

"What if he really doesn't want a dog? What if we get a dog and he won't take it?" asked Toby. "What then?"

"Then one of us will have to keep it," said Abe.

"But none of our moms will let us have a dog," said Toby.

"Yeah, what if we get a dog, then we have to give it to the pound? It might have to be put to sleep," said Ben.

"Sooner or later, all dogs sleep," said Abe.

"*Put to sleep* means killed," said Ty.

"Oh, no!" said Abe. His eyes got very big. The others just looked at him. They shook their heads.

"Maybe we could find a free dog," said Toby. "Then we could tell the owner we want to try it out. Like when someone test-drives a car."

31

"Then we could take it to Mr. Dodge," he continued. "We can see if he wants it. If not, we could give it back."

"Great idea, Einstein," said Gabe.

The Koots spent all day looking for a free dog. They walked up one block. They walked down the next. They read lost-dog signs on street posts.

They asked everyone they met, "Do you know of any free dogs?" No one did.

By the end of the day, the Koots were tired. They went back to Ben's trailer. They watched a movie on TV.

The movie was about a dog. Now they wanted a dog more than ever.

"Let's meet here tomorrow," suggested Ben.

All the Koots left. On their way home, they looked for a dog.

Chapter 5

The Gift

On Sunday, there were no more ads for free dogs. But there were ads for free kittens and cats.

The Koots went for a walk. They looked and looked for a dog.

On Baker Street, a dog started following them. It was a small yellow dog. It looked very smart. And it didn't act like it belonged to anyone. It followed them back to the apartments.

"It must be lost," said Ben.

"Maybe its owner doesn't want it," hoped Gabe.

"Maybe the owner kicked it out," said Ty.

"Do you think we can keep it?" asked Abe.

"Sure," answered Toby. "Finders, keepers—losers, weepers!"

"Let's give it to Mr. Dodge," said Ty.

The Koots took the dog up the stairs to Mr. Dodge's apartment. They rang the doorbell. They hid the dog behind them. They wanted to surprise Mr. Dodge.

They waited a long time before Mr. Dodge came to the door. At last, the door opened slowly.

35

"Hi, guys," said Mr. Dodge. "I'm sorry to take so long. I was just in the middle of one of my MADD calls."

"Who was mad, you or them?" asked Abe.

"No, no," laughed Mr. Dodge. "MADD—Mothers Against Drunk Drivers. I make phone calls for them. I ask people not to drink and drive. And I ask them to help MADD. Come on in! Who do you have with you?"

"How do you know we have anyone with us?" asked Gabe.

"Well, I can smell an animal. And I can hear something breathing. Because I'm blind, my other senses are better than yours.

"It's low to the ground. Is someone on his hands and knees?" Mr. Dodge asked.

"No," the Koots laughed.

"We wanted to surprise you, Mr. Dodge," said Ty. "We brought you a dog."

"Well, that's real nice of you boys. I know I said I'd like to have a dog. But I can't take care of one," said Mr. Dodge.

"We'll help," offered Abe. "We'll take turns walking it every day."

"We can feed it too," said Toby. He led the dog to Mr. Dodge.

Mr. Dodge leaned down and petted the dog. "Like I said, that's really nice of you," laughed Mr. Dodge.

37

The dog licked his hand. Then Mr.
Dodge felt the collar.

"Where did you guys get this dog?" he asked.

"We found it. It followed us home," said Abe.

"Well, I think somebody is missing this dog," said Mr. Dodge. "A dog with a collar isn't a stray.

"And this dog has been well cared for," he added. "Its fur is soft and clean. I think you'd better take it back where you found it. I'm sure its owner wants it back." He smiled at the Koots.

"Rats!" said Gabe. "We wanted to surprise you with a dog."

"Know what?" asked Mr. Dodge. "You could surprise me with a cat. I think I could handle a cat. With a little help from my friends," he added.

"Okay!" said the Koots. "See ya!"

They ran out the door and down the stairs. The little dog ran with them.

"Let's take the dog back," said Gabe. "Then we'll find a good cat."

Chapter 6

Kim Helps

The Koots ran back to Baker Street. A lady was walking up and down the street. She was calling, "Here, Sammy. Sammy, come here."

The little dog stopped and listened. Then it ran toward her. The lady bent down. She picked up the dog. She gave it a big hug.

The Koots turned to walk back home. The lady saw them and yelled, "Thank you for finding my dog!" The Koots waved. But they kept walking.

"Boy, we almost made a bad mistake," said Toby.

"So much for finders, keepers— losers, weepers," said Ty. He punched Toby on the arm.

"Now let's find a good cat," said Ben. "Let's go back to my place and check the want ads again."

Back at Ben's house, Abe checked the paper for ads.

"You know we have another clue to the mystery of Mr. Dodge," said Toby. "He makes calls for MADD. Maybe he got hurt chasing a drunk driver."

42

"Or maybe he was a drunk driver," said Gabe. "Maybe he hit somebody. And he makes the calls to pay back for hurting someone."

"How can we find out?" asked Ty.

"We could check the library. It would have been in the news. They have all the old papers," said Ben.

"But we don't know when it happened," said Toby. "I wonder if we could look it up just using Mr. Dodge's name."

"Let's check after school tomorrow," said Ben.

"Here are some ads for free kittens," said Abe. He had circled four.

The Koots called. All the places still had free cats. But they were all too far away.

43

"What about that cat Kim told us about?" Ty asked Abe.

"I don't want to ask my sister," said Abe. "That will make her think she knows everything. She already acts like she does. She'll be worse than ever."

"I'll go ask her," offered Gabe. "I have lots of sisters. I know how to handle them."

"Gabe! Don't!" yelled Abe. But Gabe was already gone.

Fifteen minutes later, Gabe was back. Kim was with him.

"I'll show you guys where the cat is," she said. "But you have to let me play with it sometimes."

The Koots looked at her. They told her to go outside and wait. They

made a plan. A minute later, they came out.

Ben spoke. "The cat is for Mr. Dodge. He lives in apartment A-13. He's blind. And he's in a wheelchair. You can go over and play with the cat. But not when we're there. Deal?"

"Deal," said Kim.

"One more thing," said Ben. "You have to help Mr. Dodge with the cat. If it needs to be fed, you feed it. If the litter box needs to be cleaned, you clean it. Or you can't play with the cat. Deal?"

Kim thought for a minute. "Deal," she nodded.

"Okay, let's go look at the cat," said Ty.

Chapter 7

A Cat Named Dog

Kim led the Koots to a big old house a block away. The house had been made into apartments. Just like Gabe's house.

Kim rang the doorbell. A young woman answered the door. She smiled at Kim.

"Hi," said Kim. "I'm the girl who likes to pet the cat on my way home from school."

"I know," said the young woman. "Come in." She opened the door.

The cat sat on a chair. It was a huge cat. It had big spots of black, brown, and yellow all over its back and face. Its paws, tail, and belly were white. And it was fat.

"This is Dog," said the young woman.

"Dog is a funny name for a cat," said Gabe.

"Well, we wanted to get a dog. But this apartment house doesn't allow dogs. So we got the biggest cat we could find. We named her Dog," she explained. "We really wanted a dog.

But she's been a good cat. And we do love her.

"Now, we can't keep Dog because we're moving," the woman added. "Our new place doesn't allow cats. Do you want a cat?" She looked at Kim and the Koots.

"We have a friend who wants a cat," said Toby.

"He can't come here himself," said Ty. "Could we take Dog to him? If they get along, he might want to keep her."

"Yes," said the young woman. "Let me get your friend's name and address. I'll write down my name and phone number. That way he can call me.

"Dog is very gentle," she said. "She likes to be carried. But you may have to take turns. She is pretty heavy."

49

"We can handle Dog," said Ty, picking up the big cat. He stepped outside. The cat hung down to his knees. Kim and the Koots followed.

"Please let me know if your friend doesn't want Dog," called the young woman. The Koots nodded and waved their thanks.

Chapter 8

Mystery Solved

It took the Koots a long time to get to Mr. Dodge's place. They all took turns carrying Dog. Not only was Dog a fat cat, she was a lazy cat.

At last, the Koots stood at Mr. Dodge's door. They rang the bell. This time they didn't try to hide the pet. They held Dog out in front of them.

Kim was with them. She had been the one to find Dog. So the Koots let her come along. Just this once.

At last, Mr. Dodge opened the door. Ty put Dog in his lap.

Dog was a pretty cat. They wished Mr. Dodge could see her.

"What is this?!" said Mr. Dodge. "It feels like a baby tiger!"

"Her name is Dog," said Kim. "And she's brown and black and yellow. But mostly white. And she's had her shots and she's fixed." Kim turned red.

Mr. Dodge listened to this new voice. "And who are you?" asked Mr. Dodge.

Ben told Mr. Dodge who Kim was and how they got the cat. He read the phone number. Mr. Dodge called the young woman. When he hung up, he turned to the Koots and Kim.

"Thank you, kids, for this big, fat, wonderful cat," Mr. Dodge said. "I haven't lived with a pet or a person for a long time. But you boys have helped me see what I've been missing.

"You see," Mr. Dodge went on. "My car was hit by a drunk driver a few years ago. My wife and children were killed. I was hurt pretty badly. I went blind. And I lost the use of my legs. I had to quit my police job. For a long time, I didn't want to live.

"Then I moved here. I began making phone calls for MADD. So now, I feel useful. Then I met you guys. And now I have a cat. And another new friend." He turned toward Kim.

"Life is getting better. Thank you." He shook each Koot's hand. Dog stayed on his lap. Everyone could hear the cat purr.

"Now I have another favor," said Mr. Dodge. "If I give you some money, would you walk to the store? I need some kitty litter and some cat food. Just enough until Wednesday."

"Sure," said the Koots.

On their way to the store, Toby said, "Sometimes you don't have to spy to solve a mystery. You just have to listen. And just get to know a person. They become friends. Then they share their lives."

Everybody nodded. Another Kootie mystery solved.